The Story of the Little Mole
who knew it was none of his business

First published in 1989 by
Peter Hammer Verlag GmbH

This edition first published in the UK in 1994 by Pavilion Children's Books
an imprint of Pavilion Books Company Ltd, 1 Gower Street, London WC1E 6HD

A CIP catalogue record for this book is available
from the British Library

Paperback ISBN: 9781856021012

20 19 18 17 16 15
50 49 48 47 46 45 44

Printed by 1010 Printing International Ltd, China

This book can be ordered direct from the publishers at the website
www.pavilionbooks.com, or try your local bookshop

Werner Holzwarth / Wolf Erlbruch

The Story of the Little Mole

who knew it was none of his business

PAVILION

One day, the little Mole poked his head out from underground to see whether the sun had already risen. Then it happened!

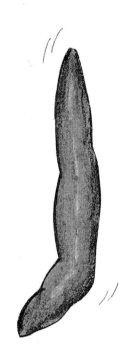

(It looked a little like a sausage, and the worst thing was that it landed right on his head.)

"How mean!"
cried the little mole.
"Who has done
this on my head?"

(But he was so shortsighted
that he couldn't see anyone
around.)

"Did you do this on my head?" he asked the dove, who was flying past.

"Me? No, how could I?
I do it like this!"
she answered.

(And splish, plish — a moist white
blob landed on the ground right
next to the little mole. His
right leg was splashed with white.)

"Did you do this on my head?" he asked the horse, who was grazing in the pasture.

"Me? No, how could I?
I do it like this!"

(And flump, plump – five big fat horsey apples plopped down within a hair's breadth of the mole.
He was very impressed.)

"Did you do this on my head?" he asked the hare.

"Did you do this on my head?"
he asked the goat (who
had been dreaming
a little).

"Did you do this on my head?"
he asked the cow, who was
chewing the cud.

"Me? No, how could I? I do it like this!"

(And kersplosh – a big brownish-green pancake flopped into the grass just next to the mole. He was very relieved that it hadn't been the cow who had done something on his head.)

"Did you do this on my head?" he asked the pig.

"Me? No, how could I?
I do it like this!"
replied the pig.

(And plop, splat —a little, soft brown
pile fell on to the grass. The mole
held his nose.)

"Did you do this on my...?" he was going to ask again. But as he came closer, he saw only two big, fat, black flies. And they were eating. "At last – someone who will be able to help me!" thought the mole. "Who did this on my head?" he asked excitedly.

"Keep nice and still," buzzed the flies. There was a short pause. And then:
"It is clear to us that it was A DOG."

Finally the little mole knew who had done the business on his head—

BASIL,
the butcher's dog!

Quick as a flash,
he climbed on to
Basil's kennel...

(And pling – a tiny black sausage
landed right on top of the dog's
head.)

Satisfied at last, the little mole disappeared happily into his hole underground.